FOOTBALL FEVER

FOOTBALL FEVER

NEXT LEVEL

KRISTIN DARELL

ILLUSTRATIONS BY LESLEY VAMOS

PUFFIN BOOKS

PUFFIN BOOKS

UK | USA | Canada | Ireland | Australia
India | New Zealand | South Africa | China

Penguin Random House Australia is part of the Penguin Random House group of companies whose addresses can be found at global.penguinrandomhouse.com.

First published by Puffin Books, an imprint of Penguin Random House Australia Pty Ltd, in 2023

Cover design by Caroline Lee © Penguin Random House Australia Pty Ltd
Illustrations by Lesley Vamos
Internal design and typesetting by Midland Typesetters, Australia

Printed and bound in Australia by Griffin Press, an accredited ISO AS/NZS 14001 Environmental Management Systems printer

A catalogue record for this book is available from the National Library of Australia

ISBN 978 1 76 104808 1

penguin.com.au

We at Penguin Random House Australia acknowledge that Aboriginal and Torres Strait Islander peoples are the Traditional Custodians and the first storytellers of the lands on which we live and work. We honour Aboriginal and Torres Strait Islander peoples' continuous connection to Country, waters, skies and communities. We celebrate Aboriginal and Torres Strait Islander stories, traditions and living cultures; and we pay our respects to Elders past and present.

CHAPTER 1

'Can you see anyone from Merridale?' Kat asked.

Her twin brother shrugged. 'Not yet. But they'll be here somewhere.'

Kat peered out the side window as their car crept along to the drop-off point at the National Academy of Ball Sports. Kids were everywhere, wearing a kaleidoscope of jersey colours. There was shouting and laughter and more footballs than Kat had ever seen. It was chaos.

It was perfect. Kat couldn't believe she was finally here. The High Potential Pathway Program, or as the kids called it, HIP. Only a hundred players were invited to the weekend camp each year. Being here was a dream come true. Usually just one player – maybe two – from clubs made the cut, so Kat was extra excited that she'd get to share it with her *whole* football team, the Merridale Fever Under 11s.

Luka leaned over, squinting past Kat out the passenger-side window.

'This is amazeballs,' he said, grinning. Kat grinned back. Sometimes Luka drove her mad, but there were no arguments over their love of football. Their dad said their Croatian heritage meant they had football in their blood.

'There,' Kat said, pointing as she spotted Merridale's yellow and green colours.

'I think I see Hani.' She wound down the window.

'Hani! Over here!' Luka screamed.

'Thanks for the burst eardrum,' Kat muttered as the car came to a stop. But nothing could dampen her mood as she jumped out and grabbed her Merridale FC bag from the boot.

'Slow down, tiger,' her dad said, wrapping her in a big hug. 'Have an amazing time.' He pulled back, and Kat saw tears glistening in his eyes. 'I'm so proud of you. My little star defender.'

'Hey, what about me?' Luka said, swinging his bag over his shoulder.

'You know I'm the favourite,' Kat said, smiling as she elbowed her brother.

'We don't have a favourite,' their mum said. 'We love you both the same.'

'Yeah, sure,' Kat said. 'But can we go now?' She saw her best friend Ava waving, and an excitement bubble was spreading through her body.

Her dad laughed. 'Of course,' he said. 'We love you *both*.'

'Love you too,' Kat called as she jogged towards her teammates. Luka was right on her heels.

Next to a pile of dumped Merridale FC bags, their teammates were mucking about.

Ava was with Sasha, Meili, Charlie, Sam and Finn practising tricks. Beside them, Crabbie, Kyra, Hani and Harper were paired up kicking balls. Harper dribbled towards Hani. They were a funny pair. Harper barely made it past Hani's shoulder, but she was fast and skilled. She faked left then ducked to the right, racing around him. Hani laughed.

Kat dropped her bag.

'Hi Kat,' Ava said as she approached.

'Hey Kat,' Charlie said. 'Check this out.'

Charlie pulled off a perfect around the world.

Kat clapped. 'Awesome.'

'Now you, Finn,' Sasha said. 'Like we've been practising.'

Finn and Sasha were best friends, but while Sasha was awesome at tricks, Finn struggled.

'Okay,' he said. 'As long as no-one laughs!'

Finn managed twelve juggles before the ball went flying sideways. They clapped. It was a definite improvement.

'Diego!' Kat exclaimed as a shaggy golden retriever returned Finn's football. He plonked down next to Kat for a pat. Diego was Kyra's dog and the Fever's mascot. He loved rounding up footballs.

'How incredible is this!' Kyra said, joining the group. Harper, Hani and Crabbie were right behind her.

'*So* good,' Ava said. 'Have you seen any of the HIP coaches yet? They're total legends.'

Kat scanned the crowd for bright blue HIP shirts.

'No,' she said. 'Can you even imagine what it would be like to play with them in the Game of Stars on Sunday?'

'You'll make the top sixteen for sure, Kat,' Ava said. 'You're seriously the strongest defender I've ever seen.'

'You're a good best friend,' Kat said. 'But we've all got a chance, or we wouldn't have been selected.'

'Kat's right.'

Kat turned as their coach walked up. 'And now you're all here,' Coach said, 'it's time to get this HIP show on the road.'

CHAPTER 2

Crabbie was glad Coach was there. As well as being Kyra's mum and a brilliant coach, she had been a Young Matilda, so she'd been through all this, and more. Coach always made Crabbie feel like anything was possible, and he needed that right now more than ever.

'I know you're used to training together,' Coach said, 'but like I've been telling you, things will be a bit different here at camp. The coaches are splitting you into girls and boys, for this afternoon at least.'

Crabbie's insides suddenly felt all twisted up, like the time he drank off chocolate milk. He'd counted on having *all* his teammates around, like he usually did. Even if they didn't know why he needed them right now. He kept a smile plastered on his face. Happy Crabbie was who his teammates expected.

'Girls, you're in cabin five,' Coach continued. 'Boys, you're next door in cabin six. You have ten minutes to put your bags away and be back on the oval.'

'Yes, Coach,' they said together.

She looked at them all one by one. 'The next couple of days will be challenging for you,' Coach said. 'But remember that it's an amazing next step and an experience not many kids get to have. You've worked really hard for this, so enjoy it!' She smiled. 'Oh, I almost forgot. There might be some special guests coming to watch you.' Coach winked. 'Try not to get too distracted. Off you go!'

Coach always did this – gave them a hint of something fun that was coming up, but then left them guessing. It was usually worth it in the end, though, so when it became clear that no amount of begging would uncover any more information, the Fever headed towards their cabins to get ready for their first session.

*

'Bags the top bunk,' Sam said as he charged through the cabin door. Finn, Hani, Charlie and Luka were right behind him.

There had been so much excitement on the walk to the cabins, no-one noticed that

Crabbie wasn't joining in like he usually did. He had wanted to be selected for this camp so badly. He was trying to be excited like his teammates, but how could he, when a week ago his whole world had been turned upside down.

We both love you very much, his parents had told him. *We love each other too, just not in a staying-married sort of way.* Now he was one of those kids who went from parent to parent. Two homes. Two everythings. He hadn't even told his best friend Sam. He didn't know how.

Crabbie heard laughter. He took a breath, painted a smile on his face and followed the boys inside.

'Cool,' he said, dumping his bags on the bunk below Sam. Luka and Finn had scored the top beds on the room's other two bunks. One side of the cabin had windows looking out at the oval.

'Check this out,' Hani said. He was standing with Charlie in front of a black-and-white team photo hanging on another wall.

Crabbie joined them, squinting at the date on the bottom. 'Wow, 1922. That's old,' he said. The other words were faded out. 'Any idea who it is?'

'Of course,' Hani said. 'It's the official photo of the first Australian national men's football team.' Hani was the Fever's football buff. 'And 1922 was when they played their very first game. It was in New Zealand.'

'Nice,' Charlie said.

'They weren't even the Socceroos yet,' Hani continued. 'That didn't happen for another fifty years. They didn't wear green-and-gold either. They wore light blue and maroon because the players were all from New South Wales and Queensland.'

'How do you remember all this stuff?' Sam asked, hanging over the edge of the bunk for a closer look.

Hani shrugged.

'You guys ready yet?' Kyra asked, bouncing through the door of their cabin, her Merridale water bottle in her hand.

'Of course,' Sam shot back, jumping down from his bed.

'Cool room.' Harper followed Kyra inside.

'Ooh, more old photos,' Sasha said as she, Meili, Kat and Ava stepped in. 'We've got some of those too.'

'Nice,' Charlie said. 'We've even had time for one of Hani's history lessons.' He pointed at the photo. 'That is the first Australian men's football team, and they played their first game in NZ.'

'Nailed it,' Hani said, giving Charlie a high-five.

'Well, HIP camp will be history if we don't get moving,' Meili said. She had her arms crossed but a big grin on her face.

Crabbie grabbed his goalkeeping gear and water bottle and followed his teammates as they piled out the cabin door. As he listened to everyone laughing and chatting, he felt some of the pressure on his chest ease. He didn't like them being split up for training, but they *were* all here together.

I'll feel better with a ball at my feet, he thought. *I hope*.

CHAPTER 3

Kat looked over to where the boys were forming lines. She saw Luka laughing with Hani. She'd never really thought about it before, but apart from the time he busted his ankle, it had always been the Horvats, Kat and Luka, defending together. It felt weird to be training without her twin.

'Okay, attention please.'

Kat pushed the feeling away and forced herself to focus on the woman wearing a bright blue HIP shirt. Kat sucked in an excited breath.

'My name's Georgia and I'm the director of the High Potential Pathway Program or, as I know you kids prefer to call it, HIP.'

There were a few giggles. Kat immediately liked the dark-haired woman.

'I'd like to introduce you to Allison and Eloise,' Georgia said. They were complete opposites. Allison was tall with red hair, while Eloise was shorter with a blonde pixie cut. 'They're our women's HIP coaches and they're running your warm-up and game drills this afternoon,' Georgia explained. 'While we do have one whole team here at camp, many of you are the only player selected from your club. So, be friendly. We're one big football family, after all.'

Kat smiled at the four girls in her line. No-one met her eye. Her smile faded.

They're probably just nervous, she thought.

'Okay, kids, time to MOVE!'

Kat jumped at Eloise's friendly but booming voice. Her whole body tingled as the adrenalin kicked in.

'Up and back. Let's go, go, go,' Eloise said, urging them on. 'I don't want to see anyone stop moving.'

Sasha started her line jogging, followed by Kyra, Meili, Ava and Harper. Then it was Kat's turn. She kept pace as they did two laps up and back between orange cones.

'Side shuffles next,' Eloise called out.

Allison was moving around, offering encouragement. She saw Kat looking her way and gave her a thumbs up.

After side shuffles they did a grapevine, high knees and butt kickers before Allison had them spread out for a stretch. As she focused on each part of her body, Kat concentrated on slowing her breathing. So far it was the same as their Fever training, just a bit faster.

'Okay, time to step it up,' Eloise said. 'We're going to do a dynamic warm-up that's great for building awareness when moving around other players at speed.'

Maybe a figure eight? Kat thought.

'We call this a zipper drill or figure eight,' Eloise continued.

Yes. Kat smiled.

'You're probably all familiar with it,' Eloise continued, 'but just in case, I'd like three line leaders who are confident they know what we're doing.'

Luka's hand would have shot straight up, but Kat just couldn't. It appeared no-one else was game either.

‘Come on . . .’ Eloise said.

Kat saw a girl in a red jersey start to raise her hand.

‘You.’ Eloise pointed straight at Kat instead. ‘You’re from Merridale, aren’t you?’

Kat nodded.

‘What’s your name?’ Eloise asked.

‘It’s Kat,’ she said.

‘Ah, the defender. Right. I know your coach loves this drill, so I’m sure you’re familiar. You’ll be our first line leader.’ Eloise looked around. ‘You two,’ she pointed at two other girls. ‘You’ll lead too. Three lines, everyone. I’ll get Kat’s group to demonstrate, then I want you all moving.’

Kat’s heart beat a little faster as she led her line around the cones in a figure-eight shape. She was careful with her timing as she crossed through the middle – like the teeth on a zipper.

'Well done,' Eloise said.

The praise sent a flood of warmth through Kat. As they re-set, she noticed the girl in the red shirt looking at her. The girl's arms were crossed, and she had creases in her forehead.

Ava nudged Kat from behind. 'Told you you're the best,' she whispered over Kat's shoulder.

'Ha ha,' Kat whispered back. She glanced over, but the other girl was facing the coaches now.

Maybe I'm imagining things?

'Jogging first,' Eloise called out. 'Let's go!'

The zipper drill was fun. After jogging, they ran, then sprinted the figure-eight circuit. There were only one or two near misses. Everyone was laughing when the coaches called a much-needed water break.

'That was so awesome,' Harper said. 'And Kat, how cool that Eloise asked your name! You're going to be in the Game of Stars for sure.'

Kat laughed. 'I don't think one warm-up session means that much. Everyone at camp is super good.'

'Yes, of course, Miss Diplomat,' Ava said.

'Two minutes,' Allison called out.

Meili put her water bottle down. 'Ready?' she asked.

'I'll be there in a minute,' Kat said. 'I just need to re-tie my boots.'

Sitting on the ground, she let her eyes drift around. Some girls had picked up balls and were juggling or showing off their skills. They were all amazing. But Eloise had known *her* name. Kat felt the bubble inside again. That was pretty cool. She was about to stand when she heard voices behind her.

'. . . calling Kat instead of you, Marley?' one girl said.

'I know. Those Merridale girls think they're *so special*. Everyone knows the only reason they're *all* here is because of their coach. She's Justine Williams, did you know? She used to play . . .'

As the voices trailed off, Kat snuck a glance to the side. A group of girls was walking away, including the girl in the red shirt. Marley.

Is that what everyone thinks? Kat's good mood evaporated.

She looked over at the boys across the field. Luka was standing with the Merridale boys. She could hear his voice in her head. *Who cares what people think? Don't worry about it!* But Kat did care. She wanted to be the best footballer she could be, but she also wanted everyone to like her.

Things weren't off to a good start.

CHAPTER 4

Sam, Luka, Hani, Finn and Charlie were chatting as Crabbie chugged down some water. Their HIP coaches, Matt and Keith, had put them through a killer warm-up. Now they were re-setting the cones.

'You and you,' Matt said, pointing at Crabbie and another boy. 'Grab a partner and two mini goals each.'

'Yes, Coach,' Crabbie said, and looked at Luka beside him. 'Want to help?'

'For sure,' Luka said, dropping his water bottle.

'Everything okay?' Luka asked as they carried a set of goals to one of the game areas the coaches were setting up.

Crabbie thought he'd been acting normally. Obviously not. 'Yeah, sure,' he said, trying to make his voice sound happier than he felt. 'I'm just keeping some of my full Crabbie brilliance in reserve. It will be blinding. Just you wait.'

Luka opened and closed his mouth like he was going to say something. But then he shrugged. 'If you say so.'

'Over here.' Matt showed them where to put the goals. 'I saw you Merridale kids when you were Half-time Heroes at the Socceroos game a few weeks back,' he said. 'You played really well. I'm looking forward to seeing what you do here at camp.'

'Thanks, Coach,' Luka said.

Luka grinned at Crabbie as Matt walked away. This time, Crabbie's smile was real. A HIP coach knew who they were!

'Okay, gather round,' Keith called out. 'We're doing some tag-team mini-games. Matt and I will be your refs. Where are our goalies?'

'You,' Matt said, pointing at Crabbie. 'Merridale's goalie. Over here. Don't be shy.'

Crabbie looked at Sam, who shooed him away with a smile. Crabbie's face felt hot as he stood beside Matt. Another seven boys joined him.

'Now, the rest of you – I want you to break into teams,' he said. 'We have two pitches set up. The team that scores stays on. The other team lines up to have a turn on the opposite pitch. This is supposed to be fast and fun. We want to get a feel for what you can do.' Matt looked at

Crabbie and the other goalies. 'You four,' he pointed at Crabbie and the three boys next to him. 'Pick a goal each. You'll stay there until we swap you out.'

Keith upended a bag of coloured bibs. 'Okay, everyone. Get ready,' he said.

Crabbie pulled on his gloves. The rest of the Fever had teamed up. They'd get to stay together while he'd be playing with lots of different kids. He felt the off-milk feeling in his stomach again. He had only ever played on one team. At least his Fever friends were starting on his pitch. They were all still together, for now.

Merridale wore red bibs and were facing a team in blue. Crabbie's hands were shaking. He huffed out a breath.

I can do this.

Matt blew his whistle to start the game.

Brrrp!

Hani started with the ball and slid it straight to Finn. He was tackled by a boy in blue but managed an outside touch to get clear and pass to Charlie. Charlie gained a few metres then sent the ball straight on to Sam. Sam tried for goal, but the goalie ran forward, scooping up the ball then passing it to another blue player, who took off.

With some quick passes, the blues were halfway down the pitch before Charlie stopped their charge, tackling a much larger boy.

Crabbie braced himself. He saw Hani and Luka racing between the goal and the play, just like they did in practice. His body settled. This felt normal. It felt good.

The boy passed to another blue player. Crabbie saw him expertly dodge Hani's tackle. Now it was only Luka between the blue player and the goal. Crabbie shuffled side to side, focused on nothing but the ball.

'What's with all the shuffling?'

Crabbie heard laughter behind him.

'Yeah, who does he think he is, Andrew Redmayne?'

'Ha. Nice one, Zac.'

Crabbie glanced over his shoulder. Another goalie and a group of boys dressed in green bibs were huddled together right behind his goal.

'CRABBIE!'

He spun back at Luka's shout. The ball was heading towards him. He dived, but it slipped past his fingers.

'Goal. Red bibs out, green bibs in,' Matt said.

Crabbie lay still. He couldn't believe it.

'I guess he's no Redmayne after all.' It was the boy named Zac again. 'Why is he even here?'

Crabbie kept his eyes down as he brushed himself off.

'That was close, Crabbie,' Matt said. 'Just keep your focus. You're doing great.'

Crabbie nodded, but he felt far from great. He felt sick, just like when his parents told him they were separating. He swallowed against the lump in his throat.

Zac and the green bibs were his new team.

'You better be ready this time, *Crabbie*,' Zac said, running past to take his place on the pitch.

Brrrp!

The whistle set Crabbie's heart racing. The ball was heading his way.

Crabbie started his sideways shuffle, then glanced up the pitch. Zac was watching. Crabbie stopped moving. Crabbie's eyes darted to his Fever teammates. They were on the sideline and he wanted to be there, not here. The ball was moving closer. Crabbie blinked, trying to focus, but he didn't move his feet. It felt weird. A blue-bib player made it around a green defender then kicked low and hard for goal. Crabbie dived, trapping the ball. He stood quickly and kicked out to a green player on the wing.

He watched the green team sprint up the pitch and score. He frowned. Crabbie had wanted to come to HIP so badly. Now all he could hear in his head was Zac's voice – *Why is he even here?*

CHAPTER 5

'There was a girl Harper had to mark in the midfield,' Sasha said. 'She was *so* tall. Even taller than you, Hani.'

'That's impossible,' Hani said. They all laughed.

'She was really nice, though,' Harper said. 'She's from the country. She said she had to drive eight hours to get here.'

The Fever were gathered on the deck outside the girls' cabin, sharing a big bag of chips Hani had brought.

It hadn't been the easiest afternoon for Kat, but she was feeling better after a hot shower.

'How did you guys go?' she asked the boys. 'It was weird not having you with us.'

'True,' Charlie said. 'But OMG, the guys here are *so* good.'

'We stayed together in a team for those mini-games,' Finn added. 'We didn't stop running. I thought I was going to collapse.'

'We managed to win a couple of games,' Hani said. 'But Charlie's right. It was massive.'

Meili groaned. 'Massive is right and I'm sure I have massive bruises down both sides of my body,' she said. 'I did so much diving. How'd you go, Crabbie?'

Mid-drink, Crabbie's answer was to flex one arm.

Their red-haired goalie was smiling, but Kat noticed that the smile wasn't reaching his eyes. He'd also been unusually quiet.

Maybe he had a bad day too?

'Kat's the real star,' Ava said. 'How do you think Eloise knew who you were?'

'No idea,' Kat said. It was bizarre, exciting and embarrassing all at once. 'It's probably the Merridale jersey she knew, anyway. It could have been any of you. No big deal.' She took a handful of chips.

'It so *is* a big deal,' Luka replied. 'My little sister – a football star.'

'Little?' Kat choked out. 'You're *five minutes* older than me!'

'Every second counts.'

Kat threw a chip at Luka.

'Well, I have some news,' Kyra said, leaning forward. 'I heard there's going to be a big – and by big, I mean HUGE – announcement at dinner tonight.'

'What's it about?' Harper asked.

Kyra shrugged. 'Game of Stars maybe?'

'I guess we'll find out at dinner,' Meili said. She looked at her watch. 'Which is right now. Let's get going.'

As the team headed off, Kat found herself walking next to Crabbie, near the back of the group.

'Sounds like they all had a good day,' she said.

'Yeah,' he replied.

'But you didn't?' Kat asked.

Crabbie looked startled. 'Um . . . sure.'

Kat raised both eyebrows. 'I've known you since we were six, remember,' she said. They walked in silence a moment. 'I didn't have a great day,' she admitted. 'Despite what Ava said. Some girls said some not-nice things about me.'

Crabbie looked surprised. 'But you're the nicest,' he said.

'Thanks. I don't know.' Kat looked at Crabbie. 'It didn't make me feel good,' she said.

The sound of kids was getting louder. They were almost at the hall.

'A boy made fun of me too,' Crabbie said quietly, looking at the ground.

'That's tough,' Kat said. 'It's a bit different to Merridale, hey?'

'Yeah.'

Kat stopped. 'There's this thing my dad tells Luka and me when we have a bad day,' she said. 'Want to hear it?'

'Sure,' Crabbie said.

'Dad says, tomorrow always gives us a chance to start again. It's a bit cringe, but . . .'

Crabbie tilted his head, then nodded. 'I like it. Thanks, Kat.'

'No worries,' she said. 'Dad also says food fixes everything.'

Crabbie chuckled. 'Well, let's go and find out.'

As he laughed, Kat saw his whole body relax. *This* was the real Crabbie. Helping him had distracted her, but as they headed around the corner into the chaos outside the hall, Kat felt a twinge inside.

A chance to start again. *I really hope Dad's right.*

CHAPTER 6

The smell of sizzling sausages hit Crabbie first, followed by the noise of a hundred kids shouting and laughing. Talking to Kat had helped, and he smiled as he looked at his friends.

'There you are,' Sam said. 'The barbecue will be ready soon. We're eating outside.'

'Awesome,' Crabbie said, looking around the crowd.

'Yeah, I'm starving,' Sam said, just as Kyra waved from a group sitting nearby.

'Over here, guys,' she called out. In the circle of kids surrounding her were his Fever teammates, but also a few strangers. Crabbie sighed. If he wasn't so hungry, he would have just stayed in his cabin with a book. But he *was* hungry, and he was at HIP camp. Everyone was here because they loved football. Just because a few kids weren't nice, that didn't mean no-one was.

His mum had taught him that. *Nothing worth having comes easily. Give it time,* she always said.

Crabbie found an empty chair between Sam and a boy with white-blond hair. Crabbie sat down, and braced himself.

Time to make an effort.

'Hey,' Crabbie said. 'I'm Charles, but everyone calls me Crabbie.'

'No way,' the boy said, his eyebrows shooting high up his forehead. 'You won't believe me. My name's Damien, but my teammates call me Squid.'

'You're right. I don't believe you.' Crabbie grinned.

'I'm a goalkeeper too,' Squid said.

'We call him Squid because he's all arms and legs and nothing can get past him,' said a red-haired girl. 'I'm Amelia. We're from Dubbo.'

'Yeah,' Squid said. 'We're helping fly the flag for the country kids. What's your club?'

'Merridale FC,' Crabbie said. 'In Sydney,' he added when they gave him a blank look. 'Not too far from here. This is my teammate, Sam.'

'Hey guys,' Sam said.

'SAUSAGES ARE READY!'

'Finally!' Sam jumped up and raced for the barbecue.

'I guess he's hungry,' Squid said with a laugh.

Crabbie stood up. 'You guessed right.'

They joined the line behind Sam.

'Look at this. A crab and a squid. A perfect match.' It was Zac.

Crabbie glanced at Squid and was surprised to see him roll his eyes.

'Jealous, Zac?' Squid fired back with mock seriousness. 'Don't be. I'm sure with some practice even *you* could progress from just running up and down the pitch to developing the *supremely* special skills needed to stop a ball flying straight at your face.'

'Ha ha,' Zac said. 'Very funny.' He kept walking.

'Don't worry about Zac,' Squid said to Crabbie. 'I got stuck on his team at a training camp a few months ago. He doesn't cope well with nerves. Just ignore him.'

'Sure,' Crabbie said. 'Whatever. It's all good.'

But it wasn't all good. Crabbie kicked his sneaker into the dirt. They were all nervous. It didn't mean it was okay to be mean. As Sam, Finn, Squid and Harper went back for second sausage sandwiches, Crabbie let the conversation flow around him.

'Attention please, everyone.' Crabbie swivelled on his chair. The HIP director, Georgia, was standing in the open space outside the hall. The volume did drop, but lots of kids were still laughing and talking.

'QUIET!'

Crabbie had seen the short, blonde-haired coach walk up, but he still jumped as her voice boomed out.

'That's Eloise,' Amelia said, leaning over Squid. 'She's incredible.'

'Thank you,' Georgia said, looking around the now silent group. 'I've spoken briefly to all of you today, but I'd like to officially welcome you to this year's HIP camp.'

Some kids clapped.

'You've been invited here because of your potential,' Georgia said. 'You all have the ability to take your football to the next level. But we don't expect you to be perfect. We're here to help.' She looked around the group. 'Try your hardest. Show each other kindness and respect. And most importantly, have fun. We all love the game, and we can't wait to see you shine.'

Crabbie cheered along with the rest of the kids. He liked Georgia.

Then, Matt stepped forward. 'Thanks Georgia. For those I haven't met yet, my name's Matt,' he said. 'I'm HIP's head coach and responsible for what I know is a highlight of the camp for many of you – the Game of Stars.'

Crabbie sat a little straighter.

'This year, we're doing things a bit differently.' Matt looked around the crowd of kids. 'We're still picking eight girls and eight boys, but you won't be playing with HIP coaches for the final game.'

Crabbie looked at Sam. He shrugged.

'Instead, the lucky sixteen will be teaming up with two players from the CommBank Matildas and two players from the Subway Socceroos.'

CHAPTER 7

It was an all-in warm-up to start day two, and the bombshell that Australian players were coming to camp was all anyone was talking about. After stretching, they had been split into groups again. First into girls and boys, then into playing positions. Kat was one of twelve speciality defenders. All her teammates were in other groups.

'You're Kat, right?' A girl with red hair fell into step beside her. She looked familiar. 'I'm Amelia. We were sitting with you last night.'

Kat smiled. 'Of course. Nice to meet you, officially.'

'Who do you think will be coming to play in the Game of Stars?' Amelia asked. 'The girls in my cabin and I were up so late talking about it.'

Kat laughed. 'We were too!'

'We were thinking maybe Kyra Cooney-Cross from the Matildas,' Amelia said. 'And Riley McGree from the Socceroos. Did you *see* his scorpion kick?'

'Yeah, I've watched it so many times!' Kat said. 'My teammate Sasha hopes it'll be Aivi Luik from the Matildas. I'd give anything to meet Courtney Nevin!'

'Oh, me too,' Amelia agreed.

'Dump your gear, girls,' Eloise called out. 'We haven't got any time to waste.'

As Kat put her water bottle down, she noticed a man waiting with a pile of footballs. He turned around. Kat barely suppressed a squeal. It was Milos Degenek, star Subway Socceroos defender and Luka's football hero.

Eloise started laughing. 'From the looks on your faces, Milos doesn't need any introduction.'

'Hey guys,' Milos said. 'I hear you're ace defenders. I can't wait to see what you can do.'

I wish Luka was here, Kat thought.

'Milos is moving around the groups today, but he's starting here with us,' Eloise explained. 'Milos, over to you.'

'Thanks,' he said, then looked around the group of specialist defenders. 'You all know that the key role of a defender is to slow or stop attacking players.' Kat's ponytail bounced as she nodded. 'Well, today we're going to take that idea one step further.'

Milos pointed at Amelia. 'What's your name?'

'Amelia,' she said.

'Could you help me out here?' he asked.

Her smile was huge as she stepped forward in front of the group.

'During today's drill, I want you to start by thinking about the basics of speed and body position,' Milos said. 'Dribble towards me, Amelia. Not too fast, okay.' He grinned.

Kat watched the Subway Socceroos star closely as Amelia nudged the ball forwards.

'Accelerate, then slow. Get your body under control,' Milos said. 'Weight on the front foot, chest forward, arm out.' Milos demonstrated.

'Now I also want you to remember, being a defender isn't all about winning the ball,' he said. 'Okay, Amelia, let's go again. This time, try to go past.' As Milos defended, Kat noticed he wasn't trying to take the ball. He just wasn't letting her past. 'Thanks, Amelia,' he said. 'That was great.'

'OMG,' Amelia mouthed to Kat as she returned to her place in the group.

'Now, did anyone notice what I *wasn't* doing?' Milos asked.

Kat put up her hand. Her heart was beating so fast.

‘Yes,’ he said.

‘You didn’t try to take the ball,’ Kat said.

‘Very good. What’s your name?’ Milos asked.

‘I’m Kat,’ she said.

‘Kat’s right. I didn’t try to steal it. You can of course, if you’re able,’ Milos said. ‘But what’s also important is making the play predictable so your team can intercept. If you put on enough pressure, eventually your opponent will slip up, or be forced to pass.’

‘Thanks, Milos,’ Eloise said. ‘Let’s put that into practice. You’ll have all done a rotating defence drill. It’s one-on-one and you’re stopping the attacker getting the ball through the cones. No kicks,’ she said. ‘It must be dribbled. Then the attacker becomes the defender, and the defender joins the back of the line. We'll have one line but two defenders, so just go to whichever side is free first,' Eloise added.

Kat loved this drill. It was one of Coach's favourites.

'Ah, here they are,' Eloise said.

Some girls were walking towards them. Kat was excited to see Kyra. She was less excited to see Marley a few steps behind. Kat grinned at the look on Kyra's face when she spotted Milos standing there.

'I know,' Kat mouthed to her stunned teammate.

'Okay, everyone,' Eloise said. 'These strikers won't be going easy on you. I want to see solid defence.'

The drill was fast and fun. Because the line was feeding into two sides, they were facing lots of different girls of different skill levels.

Kyra put up a good fight, but by concentrating on slowing her rather than stealing the ball, Kat stopped her teammate from making it through. Kyra nodded, clearly impressed.

Kat's next opponent didn't go so smoothly. The girl charged forward but wasn't protecting the ball. Kat blocked her drive and easily stole it. It took seconds. Kat saw Milos smile.

'No need to be so rough,' the girl muttered as she took Kat's place.

Rough? Kat stared at the girl. She'd just been defending, and it hadn't even been that hard!

After her third attacking run, Kat turned, ready to face her next opponent. She couldn't believe it. Marley was at the front of the line and judging by the look on her face, she wasn't happy either.

Weight on my front foot, chest to the ball, arm out.

Marley dribbled towards her. Kat accelerated, then slowed as she closed in. Weight on the front foot, she stayed focused on Marley, responding to every shift and move. Marley's movements became more aggressive the longer it took to break through Kat's defence. Suddenly Marley was on the ground, clutching her leg. A group of girls surrounded her, glaring at Kat.

'What's going on?'

Kat's heart sank as Eloise and Milos walked towards them.

'Kat tripped me up,' Marley said.

'I . . . I . . . didn't,' Kat stuttered.

'Well, it was most likely an accident,' Eloise said. Her eyes flicked towards Kat, but her expression was unreadable. 'But if you think you're hurt, you should go and get checked out.'

Marley sniffed and hobbled off with her arm draped over another girl's shoulders. Kat's face felt hot. She kept her eyes on the ground.

Why is she trying to make me look bad?

'It's time to move on,' Eloise said. 'Please say a big thank you to our strikers.'

Kyra gave Kat an encouraging smile as she walked away.

As the other girls had a drink, Eloise moved to Kat's side. 'You're a strong defender,' she said quietly. 'A threat. Just remember to be careful. Okay?'

Kat nodded, but the words didn't make her feel any better. She'd never make the Star Squad now.

CHAPTER 8

'Better, Crabbie. Now go again,' Matt said.

Crabbie brushed himself off and moved back to the centre of the goal. He didn't usually find it this hard to focus. The goal-keepers were in their own group again. He missed his Fever teammates. At least now he knew Squid.

They'd spent the morning doing a circuit of isolated drills to practise diving and controlling the ball. They'd had to stop low rolling balls, worked on grounding a bounced ball, and they'd practised parrying or knocking the ball away. Now they were in the main goal, putting it all together. But for Crabbie, it was falling apart. He'd always felt he had a good gut for goal-keeping. He loved the hours he spent in his backyard fending off balls his dad fired his way. His dad said it was spooky how Crabbie seemed to just know where the ball was going. Today, his gut was on strike.

'Ready?' Matt's voice brought him back to the present.

Crabbie nodded.

'I'll be sending in the same four balls,' Matt explained. 'Here we go.'

Arms low and wide. Light on my feet.

Crabbie scooped up the first ball, careful to keep his knee angled and down in case the football slipped through his gloves. He pushed it to the side.

One.

He turned back as Matt fired the second ball. Crabbie dived, just connecting to palm it away at an angle.

Two.

'Whoa, that was close, Lobster, or Crab, or whatever your name is.' Crabbie heard laughter behind him again.

'Be quiet,' Squid hissed.

Crabbie clenched his jaw and tried to focus, but the damage was done. While he'd been distracted, Matt had sent a third ball. It bounced, but Crabbie wasn't fast enough. It hit the net behind him. Then the fourth ball was heading his way. His heart was racing. He couldn't process what was happening. The ball went straight past. He hadn't even moved to stop it.

'Okay,' Matt said, 'let's all take a break.'

Crabbie picked up his water bottle and stepped away from the other boys. Nothing felt right.

'Okay, guys. Over here,' Matt said.

Crabbie's head was down as he walked back to the group, so it took a moment for the excited whispers to register. Standing beside Matt was Lydia Williams, CommBank Matildas star goalkeeper. She'd also coached the Merridale Fever as Half-time Heroes just a few weeks before.

'Hey Crabbie,' Lydia said.

His grin was automatic. She'd remembered him! Then he saw the looks on a few of the boys' faces. His smile faded.

'Lydia's here to help you out,' Matt told the group, 'and to help us decide which two of you will be in the squad for tomorrow's game.'

'I can't wait to see you all in action,' Lydia said.

'We're doing our four-ball drill again, but we're upping the pressure,' Matt explained. 'Lydia and I will *both* be sending four balls your way, so they're going to come faster. You'll also have to work out what save you need to do.' He clapped his hands. 'Gear up and line up.'

Crabbie was at the back of the line, behind Squid. He watched as each player was fed eight balls: four from Matt and four from Lydia. Squid was amazing. Crabbie could see how he'd earned his name. His arms and legs didn't stop as he blocked all eight balls. He even scored a high-five from Lydia.

'Okay, Crabbie,' Matt said. 'You're up.'

As Crabbie stepped into goal and adjusted his gloves, his heart started to race. He took a breath. It didn't help. In fact, his hands were shaking more.

Lydia gave him an encouraging smile.

'Ready?' Matt asked.

Crabbie nodded, but he wasn't ready. His head hurt.

Matt kicked. The ball was fast and straight. Crabbie shifted a few steps and caught it, pulling it into his chest. As he

rolled it to the side, Lydia kicked. It was low and coming fast. He made it, scooping the ball up and pushing it away. But Matt's next ball was already coming. Should he dive or try to catch it? He didn't know. He dived and managed to knock it away. Crabbie's breath was coming faster. He was still on the ground. He could hear laughter.

Get up.

He pushed up, but Lydia's ball was too close. He was barely off his knees when he had to dive to the other side. He made it. Just. Back on the grass, tears were

stinging his eyes. Matt would be sending his next football. Crabbie wanted to get up. He had to get up. People were yelling.

'Stop!' Crabbie cried. 'I can't do this anymore.'

He didn't look back as he walked off the pitch towards the edge of the oval. Crabbie knew he'd blown it. There was no way he would make the Star Squad now. He wasn't sure he cared. It looked like football wasn't the game for him after all.

CHAPTER 9

'Milos Degenek! No way, that's so unfair,' Luka wailed. It was lunchtime and the Fever kids were sitting around a large timber picnic table with piles of rolls and fruit.

'Seriously, Luka, you need to let it go,' Kat said, fighting back a smile. 'Milos said he'd be here all day. I'm sure you'll get to meet him.'

'That would be amazeballs.' Luka took a big bite of his ham-and-cheese roll.

'Meili, it's so great you got to see Lydia Williams too,' Kat said.

'Yeah. It was nice she remembered me.' Meili looked around. 'Where's Crabbie? Lydia was going to his group after ours.'

'He went to the cabin,' Sam mumbled through a mouthful. 'He'll be back soon.'

'Okay.' Meili grinned at Kat. 'I want to hear more about Milos. Did he teach you anything new?'

'Yeah, he gave us some great tips,' Kat said.

'And it showed!' Kyra said. 'Kat nailed her defence. No-one could get past her.' She was leaning forward in her chair. 'This girl, Marley, got so frustrated she pretended to fall over.' Kyra shook her head. 'It looked so fake. She even tried to blame Kat. She said she'd tripped her. What a joke.'

'That's awful,' Ava said.

They were all looking at Kat. She shrugged, keeping her expression light. Inside she felt sick.

'Don't worry, Kat,' Sasha said. 'It was an accident. The coaches know that. Trust yourself.'

'Yeah,' Kyra agreed. 'And Marley is totally fine.'

Kat was grateful for their support, but they didn't *know* the coaches knew Marley had lied.

'Thanks, guys,' Kat said, forcing a smile on her face.

'Woof! Woof!'

'Diego!' Kyra said, crouching down to meet him. The Fever's smiles turned to laughter as Diego covered Kyra in dog slobber.

Coach was a few steps behind. 'How's my favourite team going?' she asked.

'And your favourite daughter,' Kyra said, giving her mum a quick hug.

Coach laughed. 'Given you're my only daughter, I can't argue with that.'

Kat listened to her teammates share the excitement of the past twenty-four hours.

'Why are you here, Coach?' Hani asked after the initial excitement died down.

She pointed towards the HIP coaches gathering outside the hall. 'I think you're about to find out.'

'Attention, please,' Eloise called. Her voice cut through the chatter. 'If you could all come over here.'

The Fever joined the huddle around the coaches.

'What a great morning, especially for everyone who worked with Milos and Lydia,' Georgia said. 'For those groups who didn't, don't worry, there are more surprises on the way.' She looked around. 'The coaches tell me this is one of our strongest groups ever. Picking sixteen of you for the Star Squad is going to be tough.'

'It sure is,' Matt said. 'Which is why this afternoon's round-robin competition is so important. Allison will take you through how it's going to work.'

'Games are twenty-five minutes with a ten-minute break in between,' Allison explained. 'We'll have two running simultaneously. We're going to watch and referee, so we've brought in some special coaching support.'

Kat glanced at Coach. Coach winked.

'Based on what we've seen this morning, we've split you into four teams of girls and four teams of boys,' she continued. 'The lists are up over there along with your meeting place and the name of your coach.'

'That's it,' Matt said. He looked at his watch. 'It's quarter to one. Be back to meet your coaches and teams in half an hour. Kick-off is one-thirty sharp. Now, go get ready. It's almost game time!'

Everyone cheered.

*

Outside the cabin, Kat took some deep breaths to settle her nerves. Her teammates were inside, but she'd needed some space. She felt a bit better knowing that Marley was okay, but she was still worried. Kat hoped nothing else would happen during the afternoon's games. At least Meili was on her team. In fact, everyone had one of their Fever teammates with them. Luka and Charlie also had Coach. Kat was about to head back to the oval when she noticed Sam outside the boys' cabin, chewing his finger.

'You okay, Sam?' Kat asked.

'I can't find Crabbie,' he said, shuffling his feet. 'He didn't come back for lunch and he's not in our cabin. We've only got ten minutes till the game. I don't know where he's gone.'

CHAPTER 10

Crabbie felt bad about lying to Sam, but he knew if he went to lunch, everyone would ask him about training. He needed to be alone, to think. He'd found a spot under a big tree up a hill, where it was shady and quiet. The National Academy of Ball Sports was spread out in front of him. Crabbie looked up at the sudden sound of cheering. There had obviously been some exciting news. He started picking at the grass again.

'Hey Crabbie.' Lydia Williams was walking towards him. 'Mind if I sit down?'

Stunned, Crabbie shook his head.

'Nice spot,' she said.

Crabbie stayed quiet.

'So, want to tell me what happened back there?' Lydia asked.

Crabbie swallowed and looked at the grass. His cheeks felt like they were burning. 'I don't know,' he said. 'I just . . . couldn't.'

'I know that feeling,' Lydia said.

Crabbie looked up, surprised. 'You do?'

Lydia nodded. 'I'm the longest-serving Matilda. I wouldn't trade a day of it for anything, but it hasn't always been easy.' She looked him in the eye. 'You're an excellent goalkeeper. You know that, right?'

Crabbie looked away. 'Thanks,' he said quietly.

'So, was it what those boys said? Is that what put you off?' Lydia asked.

'Sort of.'

'You know, it's pretty competitive here, and everyone's nervous – it just comes out in different ways.'

Crabbie doubted it, but it was nice of her to say so. He did know it wasn't just the

teasing that was getting to him. Normally he could cope with stuff like that. Right now, it felt like someone was squeezing his chest.

'My parents are separating,' he said quickly before he could stop himself.

Lydia sighed. 'That's tough,' she said. 'You're lucky to have such a close team to lean on. I bet they're helping a lot.'

'I haven't told them,' Crabbie said. He looked down and blinked as he felt a familiar prickle of tears.

'Why?'

Crabbie shook his head. 'I don't know how,' he said, rubbing the back of his neck. 'I don't want things to be different. Everything's changed at home, and now, here . . . Besides, I think I'm going to quit.'

Lydia was quiet for a moment then said, 'You know, I played my first international match before you were born. It was 2005. I was seventeen.' Lydia laughed. 'You know former Socceroos goalkeeper Mark Schwarzer?'

'Of course,' Crabbie said, looking up, confused by the random change of topic.

'Well, if I can hold out until 2025, I'll knock Mark off the longest-serving perch for both men *and* women in Australian football.' Lydia gave him a nudge with her elbow. 'Us goalkeepers have staying power,' she said.

Crabbie knew that Mark Schwarzer was also the most capped Socceroo, with 109 games for Australia. One more than Tim Cahill. He had a poster with all the stats on his bedroom wall at home.

'You've got the potential to go a long way in football, Crabbie,' Lydia continued. 'Which means lots of things will change in your life.' She turned to face him. 'Football helps. Trust me. When I play, that's when everything is fine. We're a team, a family, going for the same goal. Your teammates just see *you*. Nothing else matters.'

Crabbie hadn't thought about it that way. 'Maybe you're right.'

'I know I'm right,' Lydia said. 'When you're out there on the pitch, you can forget everything else. The only thing that matters is stopping the ball, and you're very good at that. So, don't think. Just feel and react!'

The pressure on Crabbie's chest started to ease. Lydia made it sound so simple.

'Oh, *there* you are.' Crabbie heard Sam's voice moments before he saw him jogging up the hill. 'I've been looking for you every–' Sam pulled up short. 'Lydia Williams! Wow. Hi,' Sam said.

She laughed. 'Hi. It's Sam, right?'

He nodded, grinning.

Lydia stood up. 'Thanks for the chat, Crabbie. Hopefully I'll see you out there.'

Crabbie nodded. 'Thanks.'

'She's so awesome,' Sam said, watching her jog away. He spun back to Crabbie. 'But what did she mean – hopefully? And why weren't you at lunch? What's going on?'

'Sam, I need to tell you something.' Crabbie let out a breath. 'My mum and dad are separating.'

'Oh man,' Sam said. 'When did they tell you?'

'About a week ago.'

Sam screwed up his face. 'Tough.'

'Yeah.'

'Can I do anything?' Sam asked.

'Nah,' Crabbie said, and it was true. Just telling Lydia and now Sam had already made him feel better.

'Okay. But what about coming out on the pitch?' Sam asked. 'Has something happened? You better not be quitting on me, man.'

Crabbie kicked his football boot into the grass. 'Training today wasn't so great,' he admitted. 'I kind of . . . walked off.'

'You *what*? Why?'

'I don't know. It was all too much. It seems silly now.' Crabbie sighed. 'I've probably blown it.'

'I don't think so,' Sam said. 'That's why I came to find you. We're playing a round robin and you're on my team.' Sam looked at his watch. 'And we're due at the pitch in five minutes.'

Crabbie looked down the hill past Sam, where kids were forming into groups around the ovals.

'I need to get my gear,' Crabbie said.

Sam held up a bag.

Crabbie still wasn't sure what he wanted, but he wasn't going to let Sam down.

'Okay,' he said. 'Let's do this.'

CHAPTER 11

Kat stepped wide to stretch the inside of her leg. Along with Meili, Kat also had Amelia on her team. She looked at the other girls in their red bibs. No-one was giving her a dirty look. One even smiled at her.

Kat exhaled. *So far, so good.*

She shifted her body to stretch the other leg. She was nervous, but ready.

Their coach, a tall woman with dark hair and kind eyes, had just finished explaining their plan of attack – aggressive but smart.

'Most importantly, I want to see good teamwork,' Claire said. 'I know there are places in the Star Squad on the line, but you won't get in by going it alone.' She looked at her watch. 'Okay, I want my first nine out there and ready.'

Kat was buzzing with adrenalin. She was in the starting line-up. So was Amelia; the coach was trying her in a defensive midfield position. Meili was starting in goal.

'You're Kat from Merridale, right?' It was the small girl who had smiled at her before. 'I'm Holly.'

'Hi,' Kat said.

'I play defence, like you,' Holly explained. 'Well actually, not *like* you. You're incredible. I wish I could play like you.' Holly slapped her forehead. 'Aaaand now I'm babbling. Sorry. I'm just so excited we're on the same team.'

‘Um, thanks,’ Kat said, smiling. ‘Who do you play for?’

‘St Blanes,’ Holly said. ‘We played against you in the first game of the season. Your defence was next level.’

‘That was a tough game,’ Kat said. Merridale had won, but only just. ‘I’m glad you’ll be with me in defence.’

Claire clapped her hands together. ‘Let’s go, girls. Move, move, move!’

Kat jogged to her place on the right side of the pitch, slightly in front of the penalty area. She gave Meili a high-five as she passed.

Kat’s team, the red bibs, were facing green first, Kyra and Sasha’s team. As Kyra crossed the pitch towards Holly, Kat turned to meet her opponent in green.

Seriously?

Marley. It felt like a bad joke. Marley didn’t look impressed either. Kat saw Sasha watching from the midfield. *Trust yourself*, Sasha had said. Kat tightened her jaw.

Eloise took her place as referee, whistle in hand.

Brrrp!

The green team had the ball to start. Sasha had the kick-off. She passed to Kyra. Holly was a head shorter than the Fever's striker, but she was fast, and her defence was solid. Kyra had only dribbled a few metres before pressure from Holly forced her to pass. Another green player stopped the ball near the centre of the pitch and was tackled by Amelia. When Marley made her move, Kat was ready.

Weight on my front foot, chest to the ball, arm out.

Marley raced forward to receive the ball. She spun and frowned. Kat was already there. Marley dribbled to one side, then cut back, trying to get around.

She's good, Kat thought.

Marley almost made it past, but Kat concentrated on slowing her, trying to find a way for her team to turn the play around.

Girls from the green team were calling out for Marley to pass, but instead she used an outside touch to hold onto the ball.

Why doesn't she pass?

Suddenly Marley cried out and dropped to the ground.

Brrrp!

Eloise blew the whistle and jogged over. Marley's teammates gathered around. Most looked more confused than concerned.

Once again, Kat hadn't done anything wrong. She just couldn't tell if everyone else knew it. What if she got sent off? She looked at her boots, determined not to cry.

'Up you get, Marley,' Eloise said.

Kat looked up.

'But Kat –'

'– was defending,' Eloise said, interrupting. 'Just like we practised. Aggressive but smart.' Eloise's voice was firm, but still kind. 'She was doing a great job and you couldn't get around. That's it. So, get up and get ready, or if you want a break, your coach can sub you off.'

Marley stood slowly. 'I'll stay on.' Her head was down.

Kat had been sure she was going to be blamed, but instead Eloise had praised her. Kat looked at Marley. Her face was bright red and it was obvious that she was trying not to cry.

She must be so embarrassed.

The bad feelings faded. Kat just felt sorry for her now.

‘You can do this,’ Kat said quietly as they paired up to play on.

Marley frowned, then her eyes opened in surprise, and maybe gratitude.

Brrrp!

Kat grinned as they both raced after the ball.

CHAPTER 12

Crabbie adjusted his gloves as his eyes followed the football. It was getting closer. His team had a first-round bye, so they weren't as warmed up as their red-bib opponents. It showed.

His blue teammates were defending hard, but the reds were still gaining ground. Crabbie started shuffling side to side. He noticed people watching. He stopped. Side to side had always been his thing. Now he didn't know.

'Go, Crabbie!'

'You got this, Crabbie!'

He heard Luka and Charlie behind him.

Don't think. Feel. React. That's what Lydia had said.

The red bibs were closer.

Don't think.

Crabbie started moving his feet again. Side to side. He lowered his stance, hands wide, following the ball as the reds sent short, sharp passes, forward then across the penalty box.

'Over here!' It was Zac, attacking in opposition.

Crabbie shifted position. The ball skimmed across the pitch to the top right of the penalty box and landed right at Zac's boot. Zac looked at Crabbie. He raised an eyebrow.

Feel.

Nothing mattered except the football.

Zac shifted his shoulders. The movement was tiny. Crabbie's instincts kicked in.

React.

As Zac's leg swung forward, Crabbie launched himself to the right. It was an awesome kick. High and in the corner. Parry was the only option. It was going to be close. As Crabbie reached the peak of his dive he felt the football connect with his fingers. He pushed his arm forward.

Crabbie hit the pitch, then was straight back on his feet. He could hear cheering. Had he missed? Zac was standing there, staring at him, but he wasn't celebrating. If Crabbie didn't know better, he would have thought Zac looked impressed.

Crabbie heard a boy call out from further up the pitch. He looked past Zac.

A blue player, his teammate, had the ball and was charging past the midfield line.

He kicked to a blue striker, who cut inside and sent the ball on to another boy, who drove forward then passed to Sam. He was inside the penalty area. Sam turned and kicked the ball over a defender's head, straight into the back of the net.

GOAL!

Crabbie punched the air, cheering.

As the game continued, the blue team settled even more. The defenders were amazing, quickly forming a tight unit with Crabbie. Sam scored again, so did the blue's other striker. Crabbie saved two more goals before he was subbed out for Squid with five minutes to go.

Crabbie saw Matt standing with Georgia and Lydia Williams, watching their game. Lydia saw him looking and gave him a clap.

Crabbie felt light as he picked up his water bottle and headed back to the sideline. It had been hard, but he hadn't quit. Crabbie cheered with his teammates as Squid made some great saves. The final score was 3–0 to blue.

Crabbie was buzzing as his team sucked down water, reliving the excitement. He was surprised the highlight for everyone had been his first save. His teammates were making it sound as exciting as Andrew Redmayne's World Cup qualifying performance.

'Hey Crabbie.' He saw Zac walking past. 'Nice save.'

Crabbie waited for something else. Something mean. But nothing came.

'Uh . . . thanks,' Crabbie said. 'It was tough. That was a good kick.'

Zac nodded, then kept walking.

'Rest time's over,' their coach said. 'Two minutes to kick-off. Time to hustle.'

Crabbie stared after Zac a moment then chuckled. It was the sort of laugh that once you start it's hard to stop.

'Are you all right?' Sam asked.

Crabbie nodded, not able to speak.

'Okaaaay then,' Sam said.

As Crabbie ran back onto the pitch he realised he *was* all right. Lydia had been right. When he was playing football, everything was fine. He had no idea if he was Star Squad material, but he was definitely going to try.

CHAPTER 13

'Oh boy, I needed that.' Kat was leaning back in her chair, patting her stomach.

'I'm surprised there was any curry left for anyone else,' Sasha said.

'What about Holly? She took more than me!' Kat pointed at the small defender and her rapidly shrinking plate of food.

'I'm hungry,' Holly mumbled, scooping another spoonful of curry into her mouth.

'No kidding,' Squid said. Everyone laughed.

They were eating outside again and this time their group was huge. Not just the Fever, but all their new friends too. When they'd arrived, Kat had felt so weird being separated from Luka and the Fever, but being split into different groups had helped them all discover they *were* really part of something bigger.

'When do you think they'll tell us which Matildas and Socceroos players are coming for the Game of Stars?' Hani asked.

'I heard it's tonight,' Squid said. 'After the special guest talk.'

'But we won't find out if we're playing until tomorrow morning,' Meili added.

Coach Matt called everyone inside, and Kat ended up sitting between Ava and Holly.

'I know you're all busting to find out who'll be joining us tomorrow,' Georgia said when everyone settled. 'I can confirm I *will* tell you tonight.'

The hall filled with cheers. Georgia waited for quiet again.

'But first, I'd like to welcome tonight's very special guest speaker.' Georgia gestured to the side of the hall. Kat had guessed who it might be, so while every head turned towards the man walking into the room, Kat looked at her brother. She'd never seen Luka's smile so big or heard him cheer so loud.

'Hi everyone,' Milos said, standing at the front of the hall. 'For anyone who doesn't know me,' there were a few laughs, 'my name is Milos Degenek. I'm a Socceroos defender. I could talk to you about the games I've played, but instead I want to share a bit of my story. You're amazing young players but at the level you're at now, it's going to start getting tougher. I want to remind you why pushing through the hard times is worth it. More than worth it.'

Kat sat back in her chair as Milos talked about his childhood. Both she and Luka knew a bit of the story, but it was incredible to hear Milos tell it. Born in Croatia, his family had ended up in a war zone and then when he was six, they'd moved to Australia.

'It was a totally different world,' Milos explained. 'I couldn't speak the language. What *wasn't* different was football. As a kid it kept me going. It made me happy.' He paused. There wasn't a sound in the room. 'Obviously we did learn English,' he said. 'We made friends and eventually my parents bought a house. It had a huge backyard. I'd get up early to practise and I'd play games with my friends. Just like I bet many of you do.' Milos paused again.

Kat could see his emotion. 'That was the first moment I fell in love with Australia. The second was when I wasn't much older than all of you. I was chosen to captain the Joeys in an Under 15s friendly against Japan.' Milos smiled. 'I was a boy born in another country. I'd been in Australia less than a decade. But the coach gave *me* the chance to lead the Australian team. My family was there. Dad cried. It was our dream come true.'

Milos looked slowly around the room.

'I watched lots of games today. You're incredible footballers, but you will all have challenges to overcome. When it gets hard, remember we're here because we love football, the best game in the world.'

Deafening cheers filled the room. Kat's dream was to play for the CommBank Matildas – seeing Milos's face made her wonder what it would feel like if that dream came true.

Not if, she told herself. *When*.

Georgia moved forward and the room fell silent. 'Thank you for sharing your story, Milos. I know we're all feeling inspired.' Kat edged forward on her seat as Georgia continued. 'We'll be serving dessert in a moment, but first . . . I know I said I'd tell you who was playing tomorrow. That's not quite true.'

The hall filled with low voices. Kat looked at Holly. She shrugged.

'I'm not going to *tell* you who'll be playing with the sixteen lucky Star Squad members,' Georgia continued, 'because the players are already here.'

The door on the side of the hall opened. Kat let out a little squeal. Walking into the room was CommBank Matildas stars

Caitlin Foord and Courtney Nevin, and Marco Tilio and Joel King from the Subway Socceroos.

Kat was on her feet with the rest of the HIP camp kids, clapping and cheering their heroes. Coming to HIP, she'd been excited at the chance to play with the

coaches. Never in her wildest dreams did she think she might be able to share a pitch with Australian football stars. She'd tried her hardest. Kat crossed her fingers.

I hope it was enough.

CHAPTER 14

Crabbie yawned as he joined the small group gathered on the oval behind their cabins. All his Fever teammates were there, even Diego. The excitable golden retriever was sitting beside Kyra, tongue lolling out the side of his mouth. Coach must have come early to camp to help.

'Sorry we're late!' Squid called as he jogged across the oval, Amelia and Holly right behind.

'At least you're awake,' Kyra said, 'unlike another goalkeeper!'

‘Hey,’ Crabbie replied. He crossed his arms, pretending to frown, but the light-hearted teasing was one of the things he loved most about his team.

‘Today’s going to be huge,’ Harper said. ‘So, before it gets totally wild, who wants to kick a ball?’

‘Woof! Woof!’

Diego nudged a ball into the middle of the group before darting back towards the oval.

‘Ha!’ Squid said. ‘Cool dog!’

Diego spun in circles. Squid laughed.

‘Diego’s got the right idea,’ Kyra said, picking up the football. ‘What are we waiting for? Team up!’

They split into two groups. It was chaos. Diego made a team of his own, darting in and out as they ran around the pitch. At some point someone put water bottles on the ground to mark a sort-of goal.

'Heads up,' Sam called out. The football was coming Crabbie's way.

Crabbie stopped the ball, then dribbled. Ava raced up to tackle him. Crabbie saw Finn running forward and sent the ball his way. Finn took off. Crabbie kept pace. It felt good to run. Kat and Luka launched a two-prong defence, but Finn flicked the ball to Amelia, who passed to Sasha. They were close to the makeshift water-bottle goal.

Hani was shuffling side to side, trying to dodge Diego who had decided that chasing Hani's feet was more fun than following the football. 'Something like this, Crabbie?' he asked.

'Nice try,' Crabbie said. 'But you need more wiggle.'

Everyone laughed.

Crabbie ran up level with Sasha. She nodded and slid him the ball. Out of the corner of his eye, Crabbie saw Charlie racing in. He grinned at Hani and kicked.

'Goal!' Sam called out, lifting Crabbie up in a bear hug then dropping him and running around with his hands in the air.

Crabbie was the happiest he had felt in ages as he jogged to the side for a drink. He was about to run back out when he noticed two boys watching them. One of them was Zac.

Crabbie's whole body suddenly felt tense. He didn't want Zac to ruin this. But then again, it had seemed like Zac was trying to be nicer the last time they spoke. Crabbie chewed the inside of his lip, then took a deep breath and called out, 'Zac!'

‘Hey,’ Zac said as he walked over. ‘What’s going on?’ His voice was quieter than usual.

‘We’re just having a kickaround,’ Crabbie said. ‘Wanna join in?’

Crabbie watched a range of expressions flash across Zac’s face – surprise, caution, then finally a smile.

‘Yeah, thanks,’ Zac said. ‘Sounds good.’

‘You want to play too?’ Crabbie asked the other boy. ‘I’m Crabbie.’

‘Max,’ the boy said. ‘And thanks. It looks fun.’

Crabbie heard cheering. Ava had just kicked the ball through the goal.

‘Hey everyone,’ he yelled out. ‘This is Zac and Max. Let’s see if they can keep up.’

The rest of the game was just as chaotic, with just as much heckling. They quickly lost track of goals and teams as they raced up and down, using any tactics they could to steal the ball.

'Time,' Meili called after a particularly hilarious goal combination by Squid, Zac and Sam. 'We need to get to breakfast before the squad announcement.'

No-one argued. As they headed off the pitch, Crabbie heard clapping.

'Now *that* takes me back to when I was a kid.' It was Milos Degenek, with Coach by his side.

'Oh!' said Luka, who had stopped looking where he was going and walked straight into Crabbie.

'You have a bit of a fan there, Milos,' Coach said. 'Milos, this is Luka Horvat, one of Merridale's star defenders.'

'Hey,' Milos said. 'Have you been enjoying camp?'

Luka stood in stunned silence until Crabbie nudged him with his elbow.

'Uh-huh,' Luka finally said.

'Where's your family from?' Milos asked, gesturing for Luka to walk beside him. 'Horvat sounds Croatian.'

Luka nodded again. 'Yeah, my dad's dad . . .'

His voice trailed off as he wandered away beside Milos.

'Geez, we're never going to hear the end of this,' Kat said, coming to stand beside Crabbie. Despite her words, a grin was stretching her face wide.

'You okay now?' Kat asked, as they started walking.

'Getting there,' Crabbie said. He noticed her watching him. She looked a bit worried. 'It wasn't just the teasing before,' he added, deciding that it was time to start sharing his news with his closest friends. ‘My parents are separating.’

‘I’m sorry,’ Kat said. ‘That can’t be easy.’

‘No,’ he said. ‘But it’ll be okay.’

‘Well, if you need anything . . .’ Kat smiled.

Crabbie smiled back. With so much going on with his family and his football, he was more grateful than ever for his friends.

CHAPTER 15

Kat popped the last bit of her bacon-and-egg roll in her mouth and groaned with delight. She'd built up quite an appetite during their morning run around.

'I'm so nervous,' Harper said. She was sitting across from Kat. 'I don't know if I'm more worried about being *in* the squad or missing out.'

'Me too,' Ava said.

'Don't be nervous,' Kat said. 'If you get in, they obviously believe you can do it.'

As the butterflies started up in her own stomach, Kat wondered who she was trying to convince.

'No matter what happens today, HIP camp has been massive,' Hani said.

'For sure,' Kyra agreed.

'The best bit has been sharing it with all of you,' Crabbie added.

'Aww, thanks buddy,' Sam said, punching his friend on the arm.

'Ow. Correction, it was great sharing it with everyone *except Sam*.'

Kat was still laughing as she joined the line for orange juice. She ended up behind Marley.

'Hi Kat,' Marley said with a small smile.

'Hi Marley.' Kat hadn't spoken to her since the drama on the pitch the day before.

Marley hovered as Kat picked up a juice.

'I wanted to say thanks,' Marley said quietly. 'I didn't get a chance after, you know . . . yesterday. I don't know why I –'

'Don't worry,' Kat interrupted. 'Really.' Kat grinned. 'You might even get past me one day.'

The corner of Marley's mouth turned up. 'You can count on it,' she said. 'Good luck today. You deserve a spot.'

Kat felt warm inside. She was glad she hadn't stayed mad.

'Thanks,' Kat said. 'You too.'

Kat had only just sat back down when noise from the front of the hall made her spin in her chair. The HIP coaches were lining up. Standing to one side of them were Caitlin Foord, Courtney Nevin, Marco Tilio and Joel King. Coach Matt had a piece of paper in his hand.

The hall went silent. Kat wondered if everyone could hear her heart pounding.

'Well, that was easy,' Georgia said, smiling. 'As you've probably worked out, it's time to announce this year's Game of Stars squad.' She paused. 'I mean it when I say it could have been any of you. I hope you realise that just being here makes you one of Australia's rising football stars. Be proud of what you've achieved.'

'Georgia's right,' Matt said. 'It was so hard to pick just eight girls and eight boys. Like any squad selection, it's not just about how good you are on the pitch. We need players who can work together, with the right combination of skills.' He looked around the hall. 'For those of you not in the squad, we have a surprise. You've been split into teams to play with your HIP coaches in a fast, fun round robin. Then we'll all come back together to watch the Game of Stars at eleven o'clock.'

‘That’s so cool,’ Ava whispered. Kat nodded.

‘Okay, enough housekeeping,’ Matt continued. ‘First, I’m thrilled to say that Milos Degenek and Lydia Williams will be stepping in to help coach. Now, to make things fair – and fun – you’ll play in mixed teams, and for the lucky sixteen chosen, we have a special jersey to wear for the match and for you to take home as a souvenir. Let’s start with Lydia’s team. You’ll be in green. Could the following players please come up to the front.’

Kat glanced at Luka. He was chewing his lip. She crossed her fingers.

‘Charles Cannon.’

Kat’s head whipped towards Crabbie. He stood up slowly. Sam gave him a shove.

'And our other goalkeeper is Rylie Walker.' Clapping started as she made her way up to join Crabbie and Lydia.

'Now I'd like to welcome Kyra Williams, Zac Miles, Amelia Wagstaff and Connor Watson as our midfielders and forwards. And finally,' Matt continued as the number of kids up the front grew, 'in defence will be Danny Matthews and Luka Horvat.'

Kat had tears in her eyes as she watched her brother walk to the front of the hall and each player was presented with a green jersey littered with white stars.

'Okay, now for Milos's team in gold,' Matt continued, once the noise had died down. 'First the goalkeepers. Please give a cheer for Emily Browne and Damien Park.'

'Yes!' Squid jumped up as his name was called. He gave Crabbie a fist bump as he

reached the front of the hall. Kat looked over to see if Meili was disappointed at missing out, but the Merridale goalie gave Emily a high-five as she went past.

'Next, our forwards and midfielders. Max Regan, Sam Elrick, Marley Jennings and Sasha Parry.'

Kat's cheeks were hurting from smiling. Two more Fever teammates in the squad but only two places left. Kat held her breath.

'And finally, our defenders,' Matt looked at his piece of paper again. 'Please welcome Holly Gale and Katarina Horvat, the final members of this year's Star Squad.'

CHAPTER 16

Crabbie was trying to stay calm. After a whirlwind morning following the squad announcement, it was time for the Game of Stars. The crowd was building around the pitch. His parents were there somewhere, he knew. It was the first time they'd watched him play since everything had changed. The thought didn't make his stomach churn the way it had before. He was looking forward to giving them both a hug.

The whole squad had warmed up together, in their special jerseys; Crabbie and the other goalies had also been given black bibs to wear so they would stand out on the pitch. It had felt like a dream doing drills beside some of Australia's top players. Crabbie hadn't spoken to anyone much yet. Unlike Sam. He'd met Joel King at the Merridale barbecue at the start of the season and they were chatting like old friends.

Joel was playing with Crabbie's team in defence, and Matildas star Caitlin Foord would help them in attack. That left Marco Tilio and Courtney Nevin to head up the opposition.

Crabbie was starting in goal. He could hardly believe what was happening.

'Feeling okay?' Coach Matt asked as Crabbie pulled on his gloves.

'Nervous,' he admitted. 'But excited too.'

'Just remember to trust yourself out there and have fun. You've earned it.' Matt started walking away, then turned. 'I forgot to mention, we also have a special guest referee,' he said. 'He's over there. Do you mind running him out this whistle on your way to goal?'

'Sure,' Crabbie said. He took the whistle and jogged onto the pitch.

'Excuse me,' Crabbie said.

As the man turned to face him, Crabbie froze. He'd have known that beard anywhere. It was the Subway Socceroos goalkeeper Andrew Redmayne.

'Hello,' Andrew said.

'Hi.' Crabbie's voice squeaked. 'Matt asked me . . .' He thrust out his hand. 'Here's your whistle.'

'Thanks,' Andrew said. He glanced

at the goalkeeping gloves. 'You must be Crabbie. Matt told me about you. I'm looking forward to watching you play.'

Crabbie felt heat in his cheeks. 'I'll do my best,' he said.

'No-one can ask more than that,' Andrew replied.

As Crabbie headed to his goal, he saw the other kids jogging out too in their green and gold jerseys, alongside some of their football heroes. The kids' faces lit up with surprise as they saw Andrew Redmayne standing ready, whistle in hand. Kat's eyes were bright as she grinned at Crabbie. He smiled back. This was really happening.

The sidelines were packed. All Crabbie's Fever teammates not on the pitch were there with their families. He could see Coach too, Diego at her feet. He spotted

Sam's parents, and right beside them his own mum and dad. They were smiling. He smiled and waved back. His family was going to be different, but now he saw that this didn't mean it wasn't still his family.

Sasha was starting with the ball for the golds.

Andrew put his hand in the air and the whistle to his mouth.

Brrrp!

Sasha passed to Marley. She brought the ball under control as Sam darted towards the centre of the pitch. Marley passed. Sam stopped the ball at his feet and spun. He was fast, but so was Joel King. Joel didn't let Sam get far before forcing him to pass. Marco Tilio received the ball but was tackled immediately by Luka. They both grinned as they tussled for the ball. Marco passed back to Sam. The cheers from the sideline were deafening as the ball moved closer to the goal.

Crabbie shuffled from side to side, watching closely. The golds were inside the penalty area. Sam faked right then cut to the left, but Joel didn't let up. Sam kicked for goal. Crabbie dropped to one knee, easily scooping the ball up.

He threw to Luka. Now the greens were on the attack. Luka dribbled past Marco, then passed to Joel. Sam was right on his heels. Joel passed to Amelia, who faked then raced down the sideline. She passed to Zac. He spun on the ball and sent it straight to Caitlin Foord, right near the top of the penalty box.

Crabbie held his breath.

Kyra was inside the box, but Kat wasn't giving Caitlin any space to pass. Suddenly, Kat had the ball and was dribbling towards the midline. She passed to Courtney Nevin, who fed the ball to Sasha in the midfield.

Without slowing, Sasha spun and passed to Marley, who slid the ball to Marco.

The golds were close again.

Crabbie started to move.

Marco charged into the penalty area.

Sam was there too. 'Here!' he called out.

Crabbie turned to face his Fever teammate as the ball reached his boot.

Sam grinned as he swung his leg. The ball was low, hard and heading straight into the corner. Crabbie dived. He timed it perfectly. Both hands connected with the ball and he pulled it against his chest.

As Crabbie stood up and kicked the ball back into play, Andrew Redmayne gave him a clap.

This was the best day ever.

CHAPTER 17

Kat had never run so hard or had so much fun. She'd been terrified when she found out she would be marking Caitlin Foord. The Commbank Matildas striker was probably taking it easy, but Kat had surprised herself.

It had been a scoreless game until minutes before half-time. Rylie had just subbed on for Crabbie in goal when Sam pulled off a spectacular intercept. He'd passed quickly to Marley, who'd kicked the ball long and high towards goal. It had just cleared the top bar and slid into the back of the net. It had been an awesome kick, and had signalled half-time. Gold were up 1–0.

Their coaches, Milos and Eloise, were smiling as the gold team grabbed their water bottles. Kat still couldn't believe she was on a team with Courtney Nevin and Marco Tilio.

'Kat, that steal was incredible,' Marco said.

'Yeah, Caitlin had no idea what happened,' Courtney said with a laugh. 'I'm looking forward to reminding her about that one for a while!'

'And Marley,' Milos added. 'That goal. Amazing.'

Marley stood a little straighter. 'Thanks.'

'Okay, we don't have long,' Eloise said, calling them into a huddle. 'Attackers –

you're all fast, so keep the ball moving. Don't give them time to breathe.'

'And defenders,' Milos added, 'remember, it isn't just about winning the ball. Your goal is to make the play predictable.'

'Okay, hands in,' Eloise said.

As Kat placed her hand on top of Courtney Nevin's, she made herself a promise. She would work harder than ever and one day she would wear Australia's green-and-gold.

'Gold!' they called out, lifting their hands into the air.

The green team came out firing after half-time, quickly levelling the score. Kat wasn't happy they'd conceded a goal, but she was stoked it had been scored by Kyra. The teams had been trading ends ever since.

'Kat, that way,' Courtney called out. Amelia was charging down through the midfield for the greens and Caitlin pulled forward waiting for the pass. Instead of following, Kat did as Courtney suggested, and shifted towards the sideline. Amelia kicked, sending the ball across the pitch to Caitlin. She spun on the ball as Courtney raced towards her, forcing her Matildas teammate to change direction. She was heading towards Kat.

Kat sprinted, then slowed, bringing her body under control. She tried to forget it was Caitlin Foord barrelling down the pitch.

Weight on my front foot, chest to the ball, arm out.

Caitlin couldn't go right because of the sideline. She crossed the ball over, trying to dribble around to the left, but Kat was ready.

'Keep the pressure on, Kat,' Eloise called out.

With no way around, Caitlin sent the ball towards the centre of the pitch. Courtney was waiting. She sprinted in front of Kyra, intercepting then passing straight on to Holly. Sasha was there. Holly slid her the football, then Sasha passed quickly to Sam. Marco called out. As Sam kicked, Kat saw Luka sprinting towards the ball. He intercepted, knocking the ball across the sideline.

Brrrp!

Andrew Redmayne blew the whistle. The Game of Stars was over: a 1–1 draw.

Chaos ruled as kids, parents, friends and coaches crowded onto the pitch. Everyone was talking and laughing.

Courtney was closest to Kat and swept her up in a hug. Kat was sure her face would be stuck in a smile for days.

'Woof! Woof!'

Kat spotted Diego seconds before Kyra raced over, Sasha right on her heels.

'OMG,' Kyra squealed. 'That game was incredible.'

'You kids were incredible,' Caitlin said, giving Kat, Sasha and Kyra high-fives.

'Absolutely,' Courtney added. 'Keep it up and I've no doubt we'll see your names in the Matildas squad one day.'

'Hey guys,' Marley said, joining the group. 'Georgia wants everyone for a photo.'

The Star Squad lined up, school-photo style. Kat had Courtney Nevin on one side and Kyra on the other. A crowd gathered around. She spotted her mum and her dad. They *both* had tears in their eyes.

'This way, everyone,' Georgia called out. 'Ready . . . smile.'

'Now, we want *all* our HIP kids in!' Eloise called out.

There was laughing and teasing as everyone piled in. There were kids lying on the ground and climbing on each other's shoulders. All the Merridale Fever teammates were crammed together.

'Everyone ready?' Georgia asked. 'Say, football family!'

'FOOTBALL FAMILY!' Kat called out as loudly as she could, because that's exactly what they had become.

CHAPTER 18

Crabbie sipped on red cordial as he relaxed in his chair in the Merridale Fever Creek House. They didn't normally get together after Monday training, but Coach had organised it as a surprise celebration after everything they'd achieved over the HIP camp weekend. Even Diego had scored a peanut-flavoured chew-stick treat.

It was nice to be back at Merridale. It was fun and familiar. It felt right.

'Can you believe there are only six games left in the season?' Hani asked.

'Are any of you thinking of leaving the Fever to play just in the girls' Under 12s comp next year?' Charlie asked.

'No way,' Sasha said.

'Not a chance,' Ava agreed. 'Although I'm considering doing both.'

'Me too,' Kyra said.

'Me three,' Kat added. 'After everything I learned at the HIP camp, I want to play as much as I can.'

'I know what you mean,' Crabbie agreed. 'It will be so good to stay together, but it's fun trying new things. And there's rep teams we can go for, too.'

'And then the NPL,' Finn added.

Crabbie wanted to be selected to play in the National Premier League so badly. It had always felt so far away, but now he was getting even closer to his dream. Crabbie looked at the Subway Socceroos poster on the wall.

One day, he thought.

'Well, the season's not over yet,' Kyra said. 'And we've got Gala Day soon.' Kyra picked through the almost empty bag of lollies. 'It's Merridale's turn to host.' She popped a red frog in her mouth.

'What's Gala Day?' Sam asked.

'Only the best day ever,' Finn replied.

'Lots of clubs come,' Meili explained. 'We play round robins until a club is crowned Gala Champions.'

'Sounds cool,' Sam said.

Sasha stood up. 'Sure does. But for now, Finn and I have to go.'

Kyra looked at her watch. 'Actually, we should probably all head back.'

With a few reluctant groans, they did a quick tidy up and headed out of the creek house. Crabbie closed the door, then followed his teammates back through the trees. Sam fell into step beside him.

'How's everything going?' Sam asked.

Crabbie knew what he meant. 'A bit weird, but . . .' Crabbie shrugged. 'Mum's new place is cool. There's room for a football goal in the backyard. You should come and check it out.'

'Sweet,' Sam said.

They walked the rest of the way in silence. As Crabbie crossed the creek and headed up the embankment behind his teammates, a calm feeling settled inside him. He knew the next year would bring a lot of changes. But he also knew that it didn't matter what team they ended up in or where they ended up playing. Deep inside, they would be part of the Merridale Fever forever.

FOOTBALL FEVER

GALA DAY

COMING SOON

THE MERRIDALE FEVER

Kyra Williams

Sam Elrick

Sasha Parry

Finn Sadler

Charles 'Crabbie' Cannon

Katarina 'Kat' Horvat

Harper Brown

Hani Hasan

Meili Chen

Luka Horvat

Ava Trent

Charlie Robertson

ABOUT THE AUTHOR

Kristin Darell has been a passionate storyteller since she was a child. Whether it was making up adventures with her twin sister, or writing about the world around her, she was rarely found without a pen and paper in hand. As an adult, she made this passion her life. She worked as a broadcast news and sports journalist for major Australian news organisations for more than twenty years.

After the birth of her two children, Kristin re-focused her attention on writing for children. As an author, she has contributed to children's writing anthologies. Football Fever is her debut junior fiction series.

Kristin is a strong advocate for children's literature, working as the Program Manager for the Australian Children's Laureate Foundation. She lives on Sydney's northern beaches with her husband, two children, two dogs, pet snake and three-legged pygmy bearded dragon.

FOLLOW THE COMMBANK MATILDAS

CommBank
MATILDAS

matildas.com.au

matildas

matildas

TheMatildas

footballaustralia

FOLLOW THE
SUBWAY SOCCEROOS

SUBWAY
SOCCEROOS

socceroos.com.au

Socceroos

socceroos

Socceroos

footballaustralia